BEYOND
AMAZING

MARVEL

Spider-Man's Beyond Amazing Adventures

3 Books in 1

Dedication
For Phinn, Lyra, and Miles—MC
For Joanna, always—SR

All rights reserved. Published by Marvel Press, an imprint of Buena Vista Books, Inc. No part of this book may be reproduced or transmitted in any form or by any means, electronic or mechanical, including photocopying, recording, or by any information storage and retrieval system, without written permission from the publisher. For information address Marvel Press, 77 West 66th Street, New York, New York, 10023.

Printed in the United States of America

Mighty Marvels!, First Paperback Edition, February 2019

Buggin' Out!, First Paperback Edition, June 2018

Sand Trap!, First Paperback Edition, April 2018

First Bind-Up Edition, July 2022

10 9 8 7 6 5 4 3 2 1

FAC-029261-22140

Library of Congress Control Number: 2021950119

ISBN 978-1-368-08987-6

SUSTAINABLE
FORESTRY
INITIATIVE
Certified Sourcing
www.sfiprogram.org
SFI-01415

MARVEL

SPIDER-MAN'S

BEYOND AMAZING ADVENTURES

3 Books in 1

By **Mackenzie Cadenhead
& Sean Ryan**

Illustrated by **Derek Laufman
& Dario Brizuela**

Contents

Spider-Man

Peter Parker was just a normal kid when he was bitten by a radioactive spider and became **The Amazing Spider-Man**! He has super strength, can climb walls, and can jump incredible distances. Being the science-minded kid that he is, Peter also made his very own web-shooters. Peter takes his job as a Super Hero seriously because of the lesson his Uncle Ben taught him: With great power comes great responsibility.

Captain Marvel and Ms. Marvel

Captain Marvel and **Ms. Marvel** are one powerful duo. Captain Marvel, also known as Carol Danvers, was given her astounding powers by aliens. She's superstrong, she can fly, she can shoot blasts of energy from her hands, and she can absorb energy, too. Working alongside Captain Marvel is Ms. Marvel. The hero, Kamala Khan, is a high school student from New Jersey who discovered that she has the amazing power to morph her body into anything she wants. She can stretch, elongate, shrink, or grow! Her idol has always been Captain Marvel. And now they save the world together!

The Green Goblin

The Green Goblin is Spider-Man's most feared foe. Behind the mask he is actually Norman Osborn, CEO of the company Oscorp. Wanting to be the most powerful person ever, Norman injected himself with a dangerous serum that gave him super smarts . . . but also made him crazy! With his knowledge of machines, he's built himself a flying glider and all sorts of things with which to cause trouble. He's been stopped by Spider-Man too many times to count, which is why he considers the web-slinger enemy number one!

Ant-Man & the Wasp

Ant-Man and the Wasp prove that big things come in small packages. Thanks to the incredible Pym Particles that can shrink anything, Scott Lang can become the size of an ant while keeping the strength of a full-grown person. With the help of his high-tech suit, he can communicate with colonies of ants to enlist their help with his super heroics. Similarly, the brilliant scientist Hope Van Dyne uses Pym Particles to shrink down. But her suit includes a set of ultralight yet powerful wings and a stinger that gets the job done.

Doctor Octopus

Doctor Octopus wasn't always a vicious villain with four menacing metal tentacles. He was once Dr. Otto Octavius, a supersmart scientist. One fateful day, he was working on his experimental robot arms when a terrible accident fused them to his body. The dastardly doctor has since turned to a life of crime, controlling the metal tentacles with his mind to stir up trouble.

Squirrel Girl

Doreen Green, better known as **Squirrel Girl**, was born with extraordinary powers and a big, bushy tail that looks like a squirrel's! She has super strength, quick reflexes, and is faster than a freaked-out squirrel at the dog park. She can even talk to squirrels. For real! Squirrel Girl protects New York City's Central Park, with the help of her furry friends, of course.

Flint Marko was on the run from the police when he hid inside a nuclear reactor filled with radioactive sand. The toxic sand bonded to his body and **the Sandman** was born. He can transform into any shape or size, which is useful when you want to rob a bank! The Sandman is a fearsome foe, because you know how it is with sand—it just gets everywhere.

Sandman

Mighty Marvels!

With Spider-Man, Captain Marvel, Ms. Marvel, and the Green Goblin

By **Mackenzie Cadenhead**
& Sean Ryan

Illustrated by **Derek Laufman**

Los Angeles
New York

Chapter 1

"Watch out!"

Peter Parker's eyes widened as he leaped over a dog.

"Thanks, MJ," he called over his shoulder to the red-haired girl who had issued the warning. He held her by the hand and pulled her along with him. Peter and his friend Mary Jane Watson skirted a sandwich board and raced past a pretzel stand. But despite the obstacles in their way, they didn't slow down. They ran. Fast.

New York's Coney Island was full of people enjoying the beautiful summer day. They strolled down the boardwalk. They rode the Ferris wheel. They lounged on the beach. Only Peter and MJ seemed in a hurry to get anywhere. Did Peter know something no one else did?

Thanks to his secret identity—Spoiler: Peter Parker is Spider-Man!—Peter often found himself rushing off to fight crime. Was the Sandman stealing all the sand on the beach? Had Doctor Octopus taken over the Aquarium?

"There it is!" Peter hollered. He dropped MJ's hand and sprinted the rest of the way to the Ford Amphitheatre. A banner that read THE FUTURE IS NOW SCIENCE EXPO hung above the entrance where a line was starting to form. Peter took his spot at the back of it and grinned.

"I can't believe we're going to see the Anti-Grav 500 in person!" he said. "A machine that can reverse the law of gravity to make objects weightless! Do you realize what this could do for micro-particle physics?"

"Or basketball," MJ joked as she joined him. She rested her hands on her knees and caught her breath. "I know you're excited, Pete, but couldn't we have stopped for just one hot dog at Nathan's?"

Peter rolled his eyes. "And risk not getting in?"

Mary Jane looked at the seven people ahead of them. "I don't think we have to worry about that."

"Why worry about anything?" a nearby voice asked.

Peter turned to see his friend Harry

Osborne exiting the Amphitheatre. "Harry!" he said. "What are you doing here?"

"My dad's company, Oscorp, is sponsoring the Expo," Harry answered. "I've been here all morning. Why don't you guys hang with me backstage?"

"Do you have hot dogs?" MJ asked.

"Nathan's famous all-beef hot dogs? Of course," Harry replied.

MJ smiled. "That sounds—"

"Terrible," Peter interrupted. "I've been planning to come to this event for months. I planned to get in line early. I planned to make friends with my fellow line-goers—"

The kid beside them saluted. "What's up?"

Peter waved back and continued on. "Then I planned to study the science displays they have on the way in. And lastly, I planned to be one of the first people to see the Anti-Grav 500 in action. Thanks for the offer, Harry, but no thanks. I've got my plan and I'm sticking to it."

Mary Jane sighed. "Can't you go with the flow, Pete?" she asked. "The doors don't open for another hour. And all that running made me hungry."

Peter's stomach growled. He ignored it and crossed his arms. "You can go if you want, but I'm staying put."

Mary Jane frowned. "Okay, well, text us if you change your mind."

Peter said nothing as MJ and Harry walked toward the Amphitheatre's backstage door. He turned to the guy in line who had saluted them, and was now eating a sandwich. "What've you got there?" Peter asked.

"Peanut butter, anchovy and mayonnaise," his line-mate answered. "Want some?"

Peter's stomach flipped and he covered his mouth. "You know, maybe I do have time for one hot dog," he said. Then he left the line and ran after his friends.

Chapter 2

The Anti-Grav 500 rested inside a glass case on the Amphitheatre's stage. Though right now the auditorium was empty, in less than an hour, hundreds of people would witness this modern marvel at work. Until then, a different kind of marvel had a job to do.

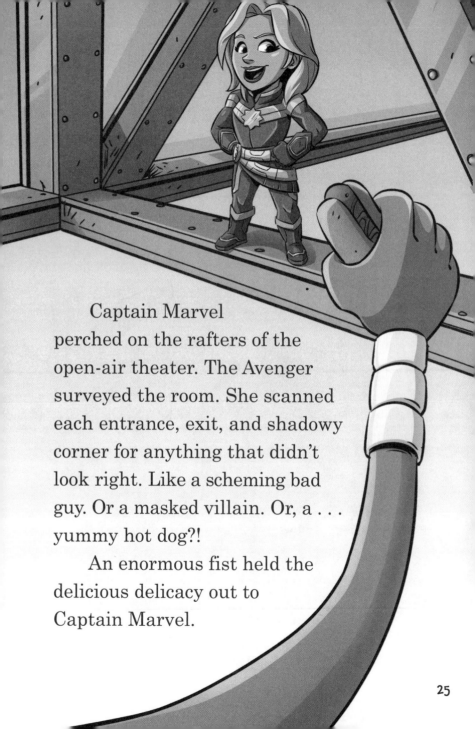

Captain Marvel
perched on the rafters of the
open-air theater. The Avenger
surveyed the room. She scanned
each entrance, exit, and shadowy
corner for anything that didn't
look right. Like a scheming bad
guy. Or a masked villain. Or, a . . .
yummy hot dog?!

An enormous fist held the
delicious delicacy out to
Captain Marvel.

"One Nathan's all-beef hot dog with the works," said a voice from the far end of the auditorium. It was Captain Marvel's friend and fellow Super Hero Kamala Khan, also known as Ms. Marvel. Her super-human stretchy arm delivered the food while the rest of her body caught up.

"Aw, you got me a snack?" Captain Marvel asked.

"That I did!" Ms. Marvel replied.

Captain Marvel licked her lips. "You are my favorite Super Hero," she said. She took a bite.

"I bet you say that to all the Avengers," Ms. Marvel teased.

"Just the ones who feed me *and* save the day," Captain Marvel said between mouthfuls. "Speaking of day-saving, let's review the plan."

Ms. Marvel said, "We scan the sky!"

Captain Marvel nodded. "If Avengers intel is right, the Green Goblin is going to try to steal the Anti-Grav 500 today. Everything we know about him says he'll either fly in or out on his goblin glider. So I'll patrol the South horizon."

"And I've got the North," Ms. Marvel confirmed.

"Time to go to our posts," said Captain Marvel.

Ms. Marvel put her hands on her hips. "Aren't you forgetting something?"

Captain Marvel smiled. The heroes faced each other and commenced their secret handshake.

"Marvel me! Marvel you! Marvel US!" They chanted in unison.* Then Captain Marvel and Ms. Marvel separated. They took their positions and waited for the Green Goblin to strike.

*Wish you knew the Marvels' secret handshake? Well, you're in luck, True Believer! There's a Mighty Marvel Handshake How-To at the end of this story.

Chapter 3

"This is the only way I want to attend science expos from now on," Mary Jane said as she helped herself to a second hot dog. She, Harry, and Peter were in a room behind the auditorium. It was a private area filled with tasty treats and comfortable couches.

"It's fine, I guess," Peter said. He gnawed on a pretzel. "But I think we should get back to the line now."

"What?" Harry asked. "Peter, I brought you here so we could all hang out. That's the point."

Peter shook his head. "No. The point is to gain scientific knowledge!"

"You can do that, too," Harry assured. He pointed to a big-screen TV across from them. "When the presentation starts we can grab some popcorn and watch it on that monitor."

Peter's mouth fell open. "If I wanted to see the Anti-Grav 500 on a screen I could have stayed home and watched YouTube," he cried. He tossed the rest of his pretzel into the trash and shoved his hands in his pockets. "Leaving the line was a mistake. I'm going back. I'll see you guys later."

"Peter, wait," MJ called. But it was too late. Peter had left the room in search of an exit. Unfortunately, finding one was not easy.

"All these hallways look the same," Peter muttered to himself. He wandered around the mazelike corridors of the Amphitheatre's backstage for a few minutes before he finally saw a sign that read STAGE with an arrow pointing right.

Peter's pulse quickened. Could that be where the Anti-Grav 500 was? Sure, he wanted to experience it with all the other expo attendees, but one quick peek right now wouldn't hurt.

He was about to go for it when something stopped him cold. An evil laugh echoed down the hall. The hairs on Peter's arms stood on end, but he didn't need his spider-sense to tell him something was wrong. He'd know that maniacal cackle anywhere. It was the Green Goblin! Which meant one thing–Spidey time!

Chapter 4

"At last," whispered a voice from behind a thick curtain that cloaked the wings of the stage. "Today is the day I add world domination to my villainous resume. Today I will make the Anti-Grav 500 mine. It will be the greatest weapon in my arsenal! My enemies will either follow me or float away." He cackled quietly then took a step toward the stage and the object of his desire. "All that stands between me and my new toy is a tiny glass case."

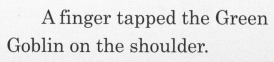

A finger tapped the Green Goblin on the shoulder.

"And a human spider," Spider-Man said.

BAM! Spider-Man delivered a mighty blow to the Goblin's chest that sent him flying. The green meanie landed hard in a corner backstage. He began to laugh.

The Green Goblin was one of Spidey's most fearsome foes. They had fought across every one of New York's five boroughs. Though he was

a madman, the Goblin was brilliant, which made defeating him that much more of a challenge.

"Spider-Boy," the Goblin said as he got to his feet. "You caught me off guard with a sucker punch. That isn't very honorable." He threw a spinning dagger at Spider-Man.

Spidey dodged it gracefully. "But stealing a priceless piece of technology is?" He shot his webs at the ceiling. "You're going to have to work with me on your definition of *honorable*."

Spider-Man grabbed his web and swung at the Goblin. The Goblin raised his hands and sent a blast of electricity from his gloves at the wall crawler. Spidey somersaulted out of the way. He landed on his feet and then charged his enemy. But before Spider-Man could reach him, the Goblin jumped onto his goblin glider. He zoomed onto the stage, smashed the glass case, and stole the Anti-Grav 500.

"HA-HA-HA-HA-HA!" the Goblin laughed. "Victory is mine! Victory is— *OOF!*"

"Short lived?" Spider-Man asked. His webs were coiled around the goblin glider, preventing it from flying away. "Now let's discuss your definition of *victory.*"

The Green Goblin turned to Spider-Man and grinned. He lifted the Anti-Grav 500. He pointed it at the wall crawler. And . . . *BLAST!*

The rays from the machine hit Spider-Man head on.

A lunatic laugh filled the auditorium. The Green Goblin draged his stalled glider and disappeared backstage, along with the anti-gravity laser.

Spider-Man did not chase after him. He couldn't. He was too busy floating away.

Chapter
5

The Amphitheatre was an open-air venue. That meant the only thing standing between the sky and a helpless, floating Super Hero was a tented roof that Spider-Man thought looked pretty flimsy.

Suddenly, a beam of energy zapped Spider-Man in the chest and his body descended to the ground. He landed safely on the floor of the stage where the Anti-Grav 500 had been.

A Super Hero dressed in red and
blue with a gigantic left hand raced
past. "Hi Spidey," Ms. Marvel called as
she disappeared backstage. Another
hero stood over Spider-Man holding
the blaster that had returned his
gravitational pull. She offered her hand
to help him up.

"Captain Marvel!" Spider-Man said. "Thanks for the assist! The Green Goblin is here and I—"

"We know," Captain Marvel said. "Ms. Marvel is chasing him now. Which she wouldn't have had to do if you hadn't messed up our plan."

Spidey looked confused. "Your what now?"

Captain Marvel explained. "We knew the Goblin was coming for the Anti-Grav 500. That's why Ms. Marvel and I were patrolling the sky. If we didn't catch him on the way into the Amphitheatre, we were going to stop him on his way out."

Spider-Man smacked his forehead. "Aw, geez," he said. "I'm sorry."

Captain Marvel shrugged. "It's okay," she said. "We'll find him and then we'll put our plan back into action."

Spider-Man perked up. "I can help, too! I'm sort of an expert on the Green Goblin."

Captain Marvel looked skeptical.

"Seriously," Spidey said. "We're like arch enemies! I know everything about him. What weapons he uses. How he likes his tea (milk, two sugars). So, I know you've got your plan but—"

"Goblin incoming!" Ms. Marvel shouted.

Freed from Spider-Man's webs, the goblin glider sailed past Spidey and Captain Marvel. The Green Goblin cackled as he rode it into the afternoon sky. The Anti-Grav 500 was still in his hands.

Ms. Marvel jetted past them. "He's headed for the Cyclone!" she hollered, referring to the giant roller coaster on the boardwalk. She stretched farther and grew bigger with every step.

Spider-Man was about to join in the pursuit when Captain Marvel stopped him. "He's got the laser and we've got the blaster that reverses its effects. Ms. Marvel and I will handle this. Thanks anyway, Spider-Man," she said.

"But I can help!" he protested.

"Next battle," she said firmly. Then Captain Marvel fastened the gravitational blaster to her back and flew into the sky.

"Watch out for the delayed pumpkin bomb," Spider-Man called after her. "He loves to use it on newbies!" But she was already too far away to hear him.

Chapter 6

ZWISH!!

Mary Jane and Harry had just returned to the line and were looking for Peter when they saw the Green Goblin fly out of the Amphitheatre on a glider. In one hand he held a glowing pumpkin. In the other, the Anti-Grav 500.

"That's not good," Harry said.

MJ gasped. "We have to find Peter," she said. "We never should have split up. We never should have made him change his plans. And now we don't know where he is! What if he gets hurt? I feel terrible."

The Goblin turned and flew back toward the Amphitheatre. His madman's laugh rang out as he tore through the expo banner. MJ and Harry ducked.

"Don't feel terrible for Peter," Harry said. "Feel terrible for us! A Super Villain just flew over our heads!"

The Goblin zoomed down the boardwalk. He flew into the amusement park. "Time for a demonstration," he said. Then he lifted the Anti-Grav 500 and *BLAST!*

The laser hit the bumper cars where two friends, Lyra and Ayla, were enjoying their very first ride. They were happily ramming the other cars when their vehicle suddenly started to float. It was about to reach the ceiling when—*FZZT!*—another beam of light surrounded them and the car returned safely to the ground. The girls looked at each other wide-eyed.

"AGAIN!" they cheered.

From outside the Amphitheatre MJ and Harry watched as two Super Heroes chased the Green Goblin and returned gravity to everything the flying fink blasted.

"Harry, look!" MJ cried. "It's Ms. Marvel and Captain Marvel. I *love* them."

Harry clapped his hands. "We're saved," he squealed. "Get 'em, Marvels!"

Chapter 7

"It's over, Goblin," Ms. Marvel said. She and Captain Marvel had him cornered against the Cyclone, right by the bumper cars. "Hand over the Anti-Grav 500 and we'll get you a knish for the ride to jail."

Just then an empty roller coaster car sped by on the track. The Green Goblin grabbed hold of it and was whisked away. "Catch me if you can!" he laughed.

Captain Marvel flew after him. Ms. Marvel stretched her limbs to cover more ground as she gave chase. The heroes followed the Goblin through every twist and turn, dip and drop of the Cyclone's wild ride. But when the coaster car reached the tippy top, the Goblin slammed on the brakes and yanked the car off its track.

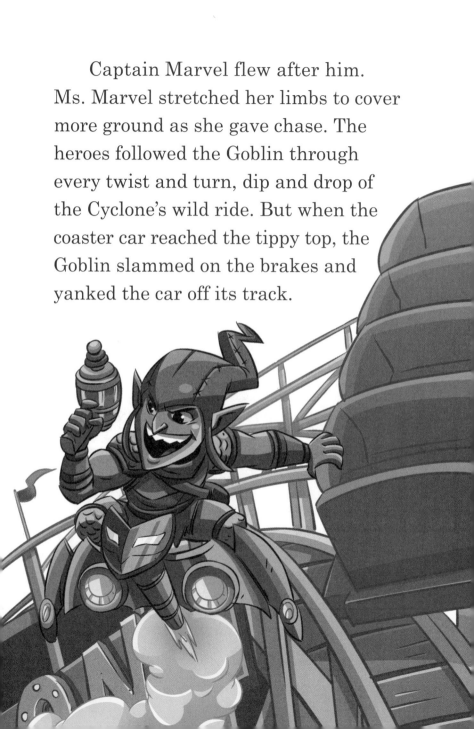

He turned to the Marvels and in a one-two punch, hurled the roller coaster car at Captain Marvel and a pumpkin bomb at Ms. Marvel.

"Embiggen!" Ms. Marvel yelled and her hand grew huge. She caught the pumpkin bomb in her fist and squeezed it to dust. "Crushed it!" she said.

At the same time,
Captain Marvel went for
the runaway coaster car. She
fired her gravitational beam at it,
and brought it gently to the ground.
"When I promised to uphold the law,
I didn't think that would also mean
the law of gravity."

The Marvels stood, fists raised, and faced the Green Goblin. He didn't hesitate. He hurled another pumpkin bomb in their direction, but it landed limp at their feet.

"Looks like this one is a dud," Captain Marvel said.

"That's what you think!" the Green Goblin cried.

BLAM!

The pumpkin bomb exploded. It knocked Ms. Marvel and Captain Marvel down and sent the gravitational blaster flying. It crashed onto the ground and broke into pieces.

As the Green Goblin took off down the boardwalk, a familiar figure ran to the heroes' aid. "Delayed pumpkin bomb, eh?" asked Spider-Man. He reached out his hands. "Maybe I can help."

Chapter 8

Spider-Man pulled Captain Marvel and Ms. Marvel to their feet.

"Boy are we glad to see you," Ms. Marvel said.

"Thank you, Spider-Man," added Captain Marvel. "It looks like we didn't know as much about the Green Goblin as we thought. Maybe our plan could have been a bit more flexible." She put her hand on the web-slinger's shoulder. "Think you could help us?"

Spidey said, "Anything for the Marvels."

Ms. Marvel clapped. "Ooooh, goodie! It's a team-up!"

"HA-HA-HA-HA-HA-HA!" The Goblin's evil laugh echoed down the boardwalk where he had left a trail of floating objects in his wake.

Captain Marvel lifted the pieces of the broken gravitational beam. "Think you two can contain the Goblin while I try to fix this? We'll need it if we want to reverse the effects of the Anti-Grav 500 and call this day saved."

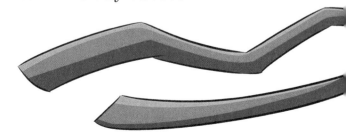

"On it," Spidey and Ms. Marvel said in unison.

Then Ms. Marvel turned to Captain Marvel. They commenced their handshake. "Marvel me. Marvel you. Marvel Us!" they said.

Spider-Man smiled. "You're so going to have to teach me that," he said. Then he and Ms. Marvel hurried off down the boardwalk.

Captain Marvel got to work on the gravitational beam. In a matter of minutes, the machine was fixed except for one thing—the battery pack was missing.

Just then, she felt a tug on her arm. "Excuse me," Ayla from the bumper cars said.

"Are you looking for this?" asked her friend Lyra. Ayla held out her strawberry ice-cream cone for Captain Marvel to see. Stuck in the center of the creamy confection was the missing battery pack.

Captain Marvel high-fived the girls. "I sure am."

Chapter 9

Spider-Man and Ms. Marvel paused at the top of the boardwalk. Ahead of them was a path of floating people, pets, and things. A corn dog drifted past Spider-Man's face, followed by an ear of corn and an actual dog. "You don't see that every day," he said.

Ms. Marvel rubbed her forehead. "If Captain Marvel can fix her gravitational blaster, she can permanently reverse the effects of the Anti-Grav 500," she said. "So she'll bring everything that's floating away down safely. But we need to buy her some time. Think your webs are strong enough to keep stuff from floating into outer space?"

"There's only one way to find out," Spidey replied. *THWIP!* He shot a web at the floating dog and tied her to a post. The dog yipped and wagged her tail.

"It worked!" said Ms. Marvel. "Let's keep going!"

The heroes raced down the boardwalk. Rising above them were pretzels and pizzas, sideshow players and sunbathers. Even Spidey's old friend Officer Ditko was hanging around. "And I thought beach patrol would be relaxing," he said as the heroes shot past.

Spider-Man used his webs to tether anything that floated to something solid. Ms. Marvel used her stretchy arms to catch anything that drifted beyond the webs' reach.

Once all was secure, the heroes located the Goblin. "He's at the top of the parachute jump," Ms. Marvel said. "But how are we going to get up there without him using the laser on us?"

"I have an idea," said Spidey. "If there's one thing I know about the Green Goblin, it's that he loves to rub it in when he thinks he's won."

Ms. Marvel shook her head. "That's poor sportsmanship," she said.

"Sure is," Spider-Man agreed. "But what if we use that to our advantage? How are your acting skills?"

"Awesome," she replied. "I did a scene from *Frozen* for the Avengers talent show. Totally made Iron Man cry."

"Perfect," said Spidey. "If you can make the Goblin think he's got you beat, maybe you can distract him long enough for me to take him by surprise."

"Consider it done," Ms. Marvel said. And she was off and running before Spider-Man could say, "See you at the top."

Chapter 10

Ms. Marvel climbed up the spine of the parachute drop. She waved a little white flag. "Yoo hoo! Mr. Goblin," she called. "Are you up there?"

The Green Goblin flew down on his glider. He held the Anti-Grav 500 in his hand and was about to attack! But he paused when he saw the white flag of surrender.

"Oh, woe is me," Ms. Marvel began. "Green Goblin, you have me beat! It's time I admit defeat. You are too fast and too strong."

The Goblin looked at her suspiciously. Ms. Marvel held her breath. Then the Goblin settled into his glider. "And too clever," he added. "Don't forget too clever."

"And too clever," she agreed eagerly. She looked around. No Spider-Man yet. "You really are just so good at this bad guy thing. You're very—"

"Inspiring?" he asked.

"Totally inspiring!" Ms. Marvel cried. Still no Spidey. She continued to stall. "In fact, your, uh, success is making me consider a career change. Yeah, that's it. I want to be a bad guy!"

"Really?" The Goblin asked. "*I* made *you* want to be a villain?"

Suddenly, the Goblin felt a tap on his shoulder. He spun around to see Spider-Man hanging upside down behind him. "Nah," Spidey said. "But *she* did make *me* want to take acting lessons. Also, you have to stop falling for this."

WHAM!

Spider-Man knocked the Green Goblin out cold and straight off his glider. The bad guy flew down the boardwalk and landed in a car on the Wonder Wheel, where Officer Stanley and the NYPD were waiting.

"Nice job, Spider-Man," Ms. Marvel said. He did not reply. "Spider-Man?" She looked around the parachute jump. Spidey wasn't there. Then she looked up and gasped. Spider-Man was holding the Anti-Grav 500 and floating up into the sky!

"I got the laser!" he hollered. "Unfortunately, it got me, too."

"Hang tight," Ms. Marvel called. She climbed to the top of the parachute jump and stretched her body as long as she could, reaching for Spider-Man's foot. She almost had hold of his toes when a gust

of wind came up from the ocean and
blew Spider-Man away.

"Okay, so that wasn't good," he said
to himself. He looked up at the sky and
gulped. "Outer space, huh? Never really
wanted to go there. Doesn't seem so fun!"

A bird flying nearby did a double
take when she saw the floating hero.
Spider-Man whistled to her. "Hey, little
birdie, think I could hitch a ride back
down to the boardwalk? Give me a lift
and I'll spring for some peanuts."

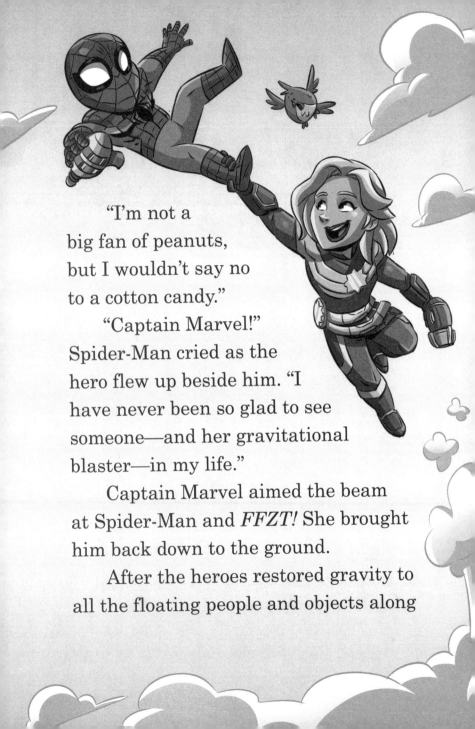

"I'm not a
big fan of peanuts,
but I wouldn't say no
to a cotton candy."

"Captain Marvel!"
Spider-Man cried as the
hero flew up beside him. "I
have never been so glad to see
someone—and her gravitational
blaster—in my life."

Captain Marvel aimed the beam
at Spider-Man and *FFZT!* She brought
him back down to the ground.

After the heroes restored gravity to
all the floating people and objects along

the boardwalk, they returned the Anti-Grav 500 to the science expo.

"Thanks for your help today, Spider-Man," Captain Marvel said. "I'm sorry I started out so stuck on my plan. Though having a plan is an important part of dealing with a problem, sometimes things change and we have to be able to change with them. Who knows? Sometimes the plan can get even better!"

"Believe it or not," said Spidey, "I totally understand." He thought of MJ and Harry and how he could have been more flexible with his own plan.

Ms. Marvel bounced excitedly. "Because you were such an awesome part of the team today, we thought we'd make you an honorary Marvel," she said. "Want to learn our handshake?"

Spider-Man gasped. The Marvels grinned. "Do I?!" he replied.

The trio wasted no time getting to work. Before long they perfected the handshake, complete with a special added twist.

"Marvel me. Marvel you. Marvel us! Excelsior!" they cried.

Captain Marvel threw her arm around Spider-Man's shoulder. "Now, about that cotton candy . . ."

"Peter!" Mary Jane cried. She and Harry were standing outside the gates of Luna Park when she saw her missing friend approach. She ran to him and hugged him hard. "We are so glad to see you!"

"Yeah," Harry agreed. "Next time you storm off, make sure the Green Goblin isn't flying around zapping people with an anti-gravity laser. Okay?"

Peter laughed. "Okay," he agreed.

MJ pulled away and looked at the ground. "We're sorry we asked you to change your plans today," she said. "We knew how excited you were to see the Anti-Grav 500 and it stinks that you missed it."

"Oh, I got to see how it works," Peter said.

"Yeah, the Goblin put on quite a show," Harry agreed. "But really, Pete. We are sorry for messing up your plan."

Peter regarded his friends. "Thanks, guys, but I'm sorry, too," he said. "Things don't always go according to plan and that's okay. I'll try to be better at *going with the flow* from now on."

MJ linked her arm through Peter's. "Well, we've got a couple hours left before we have to head home. What do you want to do now?"

Peter thought about it. He shrugged and smiled. "I don't know," he said. "Let's just see what happens."

Buggin' Out!

With Spider-Man,
Ant-Man, the Wasp, and
Doctor Octopus

By **Mackenzie Cadenhead**
& Sean Ryan

Illustrated by **Derek Laufman**

Los Angeles
New York

Chapter 1

"Jaeger."

"Bacharach."

"Choi."

"Schulte."

The students whose names were
called stood beside their team captains,
Missy Ruiz and Flash Thompson.

"I'll take Buck next," Missy said. She
gave Buck a high five.

"Powell's with me," said Flash.
Powell joined his cheering teammates.

"That leaves Murphy and Parker,"
Coach Bennett said. He pointed at the

two boys standing on the sidelines of the basketball court.

Donnie Murphy looked at his feet. He didn't like basketball. He didn't like sports of any kind. He hoped that if he didn't make eye contact he would never be picked.

Peter Parker, on the other hand, was eager to join a team. While Peter had the reputation of being an uncoordinated brainiac, he secretly loved playing sports. He secretly loved doing anything athletic. Because secretly, he was the arachnid acrobat known as Spider-Man!

In order to keep his Super Hero identity secret, Peter always had to play down his amazing skills. But today he just wanted to participate. Even if he only used ten percent of his ability, Peter knew he could be the star of Midtown High's PE program. And after years of being picked last, he wanted to shine.

Peter smiled at Missy as she considered her choice. *Pick me*, he thought. *Pick me!*

"Murphy," Missy said.

Peter's shoulders slumped.

"I guess Parker's with us," said Flash.

Peter straightened up. He could still show them what he could do! But as he went to join his team, Flash blocked his path.

Flash was the most athletic boy at school. He was big and strong, and though he might not have been at the top of any class other than Gym, Peter was eager to hear his words of wisdom. "Why don't you sit this one out, Parker?" Flash said. "Hold up the wall with Murphy while the rest of us athletes play four-on-four. We'll make sure the ball never comes near you."

This was not the pep talk Peter was hoping for. He opened his mouth to tell Flash that he actually wanted to play. But before he could speak, Peter's spider-sense began to tingle. A basketball was about to hit the back of his head!

Peter's mind raced. What should he do? If he spun around and caught the ball, everyone would see his quick reflexes. Then they'd all want him on their team! But if he caught a ball he clearly couldn't see, his classmates might start to wonder how he did it. And his secret identity as Spider-Man would be compromised.

Could he risk it? No. The only choice was to let the ball hit him. Peter braced for impact.

Suddenly, Flash reached out and caught the ball. "That was a close one," he said. "Like I was saying, stay out of our way, Parker. Wouldn't want that big brain of yours to get hurt."

Flash laughed and joined the rest of the boys and girls on the court. Coach Bennett blew his whistle and started the game. Peter walked over to the sideline where Donnie Murphy had already sat down.

Donnie relaxed against the gymnasium wall. "Lucky we don't have to play, huh?" he said.

Peter watched as Flash tossed the basketball into the net. *SWISH!*

"Yeah." Peter sighed. "Lucky us."

Chapter 2

Despite the morning's basketball bust, Peter's afternoon was looking up. It was time for the school science fair. This year it was being held at Empire State University, and the real scientists who worked there would be the judges. At stake was the coveted Big Apple Science Trophy. Peter knew the competition would be fierce. But he also knew how hard he had worked on his project. He was confident he had a shot at winning the top prize.

"I'd like to see Flash Thompson do something like this," Peter mumbled to himself, steaming all over again as he remembered how Flash had sunk shot after shot in PE.

"What was that?" asked Aunt May. She had come all the way from Queens to see her nephew in scientific action.

"I said, uh, thanks for coming to this," Peter replied.

"I wouldn't miss it for anything," said Aunt May. "Although I must admit, I don't entirely understand what

your project is about." She pointed to the large tub of water that Peter was wheeling into the science fair room. Inside the tub were four long metal poles connected by wires.

"I call it *A New Kind of Current*," Peter said. "I'm showing how we can create electricity by using water's natural movement. I got the idea after we went to the beach and the waves kept pushing me back out of the water. There's a lot of power in those waves! So for my project I figured out how to take that power and turn it into electrical energy."

Aunt May raised her eyebrows. "All I think about at the beach is who the bad guy is in the Agatha Twisty mystery I'm reading." She squeezed her nephew's arm. "Peter, I am very impressed."

Peter blushed. For a moment all thoughts of Flash Thompson and basketball were forgotten. Until . . .

"Excuse me. Coming through!" said Flash. His shirt was untucked and his hair was a mess. The normally cucumber-cool athlete was anything but as he stumbled into the fair room carrying a glass case and some index cards.

Flash dumped his stuff on the table next to Peter's. Peter rolled his eyes. He wondered what on earth Flash Thompson could be presenting at the science fair. How many basketball players it takes to screw in a lightbulb?

"Oh, hey, Parker," Flash said, as he glanced up from his project. "I had to run here from basketball practice. I was worried I'd be late." Flash looked around. Though it was cool in the fair room, he continued to sweat. "Yikes, there's a lot of smart stuff in here."

Peter smiled. "There sure is."

"Wow," said Flash. "I didn't know water could make electricity. Your project looks great!"

"Thanks," Peter said. He looked at the jumble of papers on Flash's table. He knew he was being unkind, but he was still hurt by Flash's rude behavior in gym class that morning. It felt good to be better than Flash at something. Trying not to snicker, Peter asked, "What's your project?"

Flash showed Peter his note cards. To Peter's surprise, they had drawings of different types of ants and captions about their special skills. Inside the glass case was a habitat with hundreds of ants. Peter was impressed.

"I call it *Heavy Lifting: The Ant*," Flash said. "I like ants, you know? They're, like, superstrong."

Peter couldn't believe it. "It looks like you put a lot of effort into your project," he said.

"I've been working on this for weeks," Flash replied.

As Flash set up his project, Peter returned to his table and pouted. If Peter wasn't welcome to play basketball, then Flash shouldn't be able to do science. Peter thought he'd rather be in a big Super Hero fight than watch Flash beat him at the science fair, too.

Little did he know his wish was about to be granted.

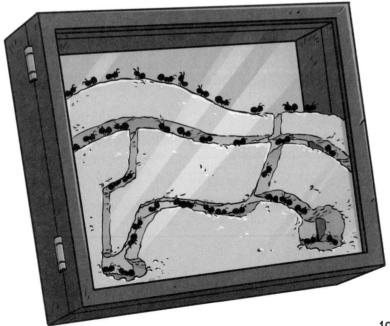

Chapter 3

In another corner of Empire State University, Hope Van Dyne stood before a giant husk of corn in the lab where she and Scott Lang worked. She had encountered enormous vegetables other times when she shrank down to her Super Hero form, the Wasp. But in those cases, the vegetables were normal size, and Hope was super-small. Today was different. Hope was currently regular-human size. And this corn was as big as a minivan.

"It worked!" Hope said. She clapped her hands in excitement. "We've successfully altered the Pym Particles into Gigantor Particles. Usually they allow us to shrink down to insect size, but today we've made them do the opposite—grow organic material bigger! This could be the answer to world hunger. Imagine if we could grow fields of giant corn. Or apples."

"Or pizza!" Scott chimed in. Scott was Hope's partner in the lab—and in battle—as the Super Hero Ant-Man.

"Yes, Scott," Hope said. She rolled her eyes. "Or pizza." She walked over to the particle spectrometer at the far end of their lab. She pulled a canister from its base and made sure the lid was shut tight. "This is just our first test. We still have to make sure the organic compounds maintain their atomic structure when enlarged."

"Which is science talk for big corn same as little corn?" Scott asked.

Hope nodded and tossed him the canister.

"That canister contains the only collection of Gigantor Particles that can enlarge organic matter," she explained. "This is one of the most important scientific breakthroughs in generations. We have to keep it safe. In other words, don't open it."

Scott fastened the canister to the holster of his Ant-Man suit. "You can count on me," he said. "Or my name isn't—"

BOOM!

The door to the lab burst open and a menacing man with four metal tentacles pushed through the doorway.

"Doctor Octopus!" Scott shouted.

A tentacle shot into the room and snatched the canister containing the Gigantor Particles from Ant-Man's suit.

"The one and only," the Super Villain said as an evil grin spread across his face.

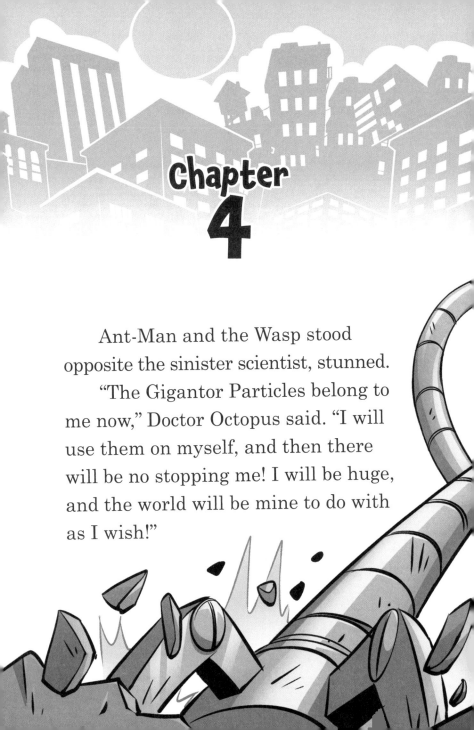

Chapter 4

Ant-Man and the Wasp stood opposite the sinister scientist, stunned.

"The Gigantor Particles belong to me now," Doctor Octopus said. "I will use them on myself, and then there will be no stopping me! I will be huge, and the world will be mine to do with as I wish!"

Doc Ock's metal arms flailed around the laboratory. Wasp and Ant-Man jumped out of the way just as one crashed down between them. Ant-Man shrank down to his ant size, while the full-size Wasp flew over to confront the villain.

"The Gigantor Particles are experimental," she said, trying to stay calm. "We don't know how they work on humans yet. You're putting yourself in danger if you open that canister."

"Silly insect," Doc Ock said. "I don't need you to finish this work. I have the superior scientific mind. I will make these particles perform perfectly. And then I will squash you like the bugs you are."

Doc Ock froze. "Wait, there's only one of you? I thought there were two. Where did the other one go? Where is the little ant boy?"

"That's Ant-MAN to you!" a tiny voice said from the tip of a tentacle's pincer. It held the canister of Gigantor Particles. Ant-Man pried the claw open and the canister fell to the ground.

"Noooo!" Doctor Octopus cried. He reached for the plummeting particles, but he was too slow.

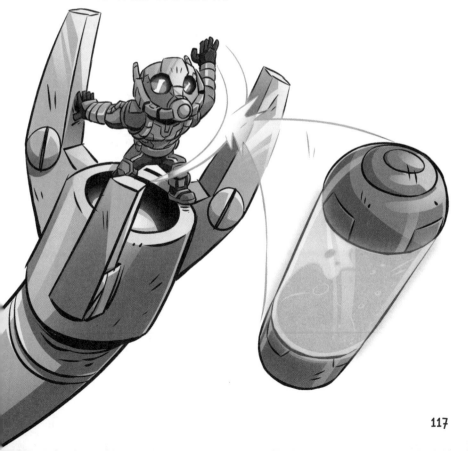

"Gotcha," the Wasp said. She'd shrunk down now, too. She caught the canister before it hit the floor. Then she flew out of the laboratory with it.

Ant-Man followed on foot.

Doctor Octopus came right behind him.

The chase was on!

Chapter 5

Three judges stood before Flash's ant project.

"Sometimes even the strongest ant needs some help," Flash said. "Sure, he can lift up to five thousand times his own weight, but when there's something that's too heavy to carry on his own, that little guy will call on his friends to help him out. I tested this by leaving out a superheavy Cheerio, and sure enough a group of five ants worked together to carry it away.

I guess you could say ants have got brains *and* brawn!" The science fair judges laughed. Flash smiled. Peter frowned.

This was really happening. Flash Thompson was doing well at science. And worse, Peter himself was interested in Flash's project. Peter knew he shouldn't be so annoyed. Assuming Flash wouldn't be good at schoolwork just because he was good

at sports was unfair. Just as unfair
as Flash thinking Peter couldn't play
basketball because he was smart. But
Peter didn't care about fairness right
now. He just wanted the judges to stop
paying attention to Flash.

Which they did, the moment
Doctor Octopus came raging through
the door. Panic ensued at the sight of
the metal-tentacled menace.

"Give me those particles!" Doc Ock
cried.

Ant-Man was right beside him. "What's the magic word?" he asked.

Doctor Octopus swung a metal arm.

Ant-Man ducked. "Please," the tiniest Avenger said. "The magic word is *please*."

"Enough of this foolishness!" said Doctor Octopus. "I am the superior scientist! The altered Pym Particles will be mine. And you will give them to me now!"

Peter was wondering what particles they were talking about when he noticed a lone canister floating through the air. It moved with direction and purpose, as if someone very small was flying it. Suddenly it dipped down and shot past Aidan Taylor's homemade volcano before disappearing into Reilly First's dry-ice project.

Peter knew what he had to do.

As scientists and students scattered, Peter grabbed Aunt May and pushed her out the door to safety. Amid the chaos, he disappeared back into the crowd. Peter hated leaving his aunt, but he needed to help. He needed to find an empty classroom to change. He needed to become *the amazing Spider-Man!*

Chapter 6

Doctor Octopus slammed his
tentacles down hard on the floor.
Ant-Man weaved between them. He got
in close to Doc Ock's body and slammed
against his chest with all his might. The
mad scientist stumbled backward.
Ant-Man was about to land another
punch when a metal arm
swiped right and knocked
him through the air.

Ant-Man landed in the jaws of a pincer. The menacing metal claw began to close. Ant-Man was as good as squashed until . . .

FWOOSH!

The Wasp swooped in. She lifted Ant-Man out of the tentacle's grasp and flew him to safety.

"I've really got to get me some wings," Ant-Man said.

"You're welcome," replied the Wasp.

"RAAARRRR!" roared Doctor Octopus. He grabbed hold of the nearest table and flipped it. Science projects flew everywhere, including Reilly's dry-ice experiment. The canister of Gigantor Particles rolled out from the mist.

"The particles!" the Wasp cried. She dropped Ant-Man at the foot of the artificial volcano and flew as fast as she could for the canister.

She reached out a hand.

She almost had it when— *SLAM!* One of Doc Ock's tentacles swatted her aside.

The evil scientist lifted the canister. "Victory," he cried. "Victory is mine!"

The Wasp called to Ant-Man, "I think it's time we let Doctor Octopus know what Pym Particles actually feel like."

"Roger that," said Ant-Man. He took a gas balloon filled with shrinking Pym Particles from his utility belt and hurled it at the Super Villain.

Just then, Spider-Man swung onto the scene. He had timed his entrance perfectly. The trajectory of his swing was right on track. He knocked Doctor Octopus off his feet and sent them both flying . . . right into Ant-Man's shrinking balloon!

BURST!

Spider-Man, Doctor Octopus, and the canister of Gigantor Particles shrank down to insect size. They tumbled into the Amanat cousins' group project, landing inside the jaws of a Venus flytrap!

Spider-Man lay on his side, face-to-face with Doctor Octopus. The Venus flytrap began to close.

"I don't know what's worse," Spidey said. "The fact that I'm the size of a lima bean and I'm about to be eaten by a plant, or the fishy breath on *you*." He waved his hand in front of his nose. "Is that why they call you Doctor *Octopus*? Pee-yew!"

"Enough, you bothersome bug!"
Doc Ock shoved the web-slinger aside.
He spotted the canister of Gigantor
Particles caught between two of the
flytrap's teeth. His now-tiny metal
tentacles lifted him toward it, but
before he could reach out, Spider-Man
tackled him from behind.

"I don't know what those particles
do," Spidey said. "But I'm guessing
they're not for you!" He webbed Doc
Ock's metal extremities together and
hurled him toward the ceiling. The
fearsome foe flew up and out of the
plant's jaws, taking Spider-Man with
him. They crash-landed on top of a
table.

"You fool!" Doctor Octopus cried.
"The canister will be crushed!"

Ant-Man ran up beside them. "Octopuppy's right," he said. "If those particles are released, there's going to be a giant man-eating plant in the middle of Manhattan."

While Doctor Octopus and Ant-Man stared in horror at the flytrap's closing jaws, Spider-Man stared in awe at his fellow Super Hero. "Excuse me, Ant-Man," he said. "Hi, I'm your friendly neighborhood Spider-Man, and can I just say I love your work with the Avengers? Seriously, this is *huge*. Or should I say *tiny*? You know, because we're small?" He laughed at his own joke. "Anyway, I've always wanted to team up with you. And now you're here, and I'm here, so maybe we can—" Spider-Man paused. "I'm sorry, did

you say 'giant man-eating plant'? The particles make things bigger?"

Ant-Man nodded.

Spidey hung his head. "My bad."

The trio watched as the plant's leaves tightened and the canister was about to burst.

"I can't look," Ant-Man said, turning away.

Suddenly, the Wasp swooped in, grabbed the canister, and saved the day.

She landed beside Ant-Man. He gave her a high five. "I knew we'd be okay!" he exclaimed.

"Enough! The particles will be mine!" Doctor Octopus yelled. His tentacles moved into action, each one knocking a hero aside. The canister flew into the air once more. Doc Ock reached for it, but Spider-Man's web snatched it first.

As he handed the canister to the Wasp, Spider-Man said, "May I just say it's a real honor to be fighting alongside— Oof!"

A tentacle grabbed Spider-Man and hurled him into the air. The Wasp jumped out of the path of another. "Ant-Man," she hollered. "Go long!"

Ant-Man took off, and the Wasp threw the canister. It sailed over Doctor Octopus's head and landed right in Ant-Man's arms.

Ant-Man climbed through a project about climate change (*CO$_2$ Much?*) and ran past a poster on running (*Fartlek Training: It's Not Just a Silly Name!*). But Doc Ock was gaining on him. By the time Ant-Man reached the base of the baking-soda volcano, the brilliant bad guy was on his heels.

"Ant-Man," Spider-Man called from the top of the volcano. "Up here!" But just as Ant-Man launched the canister, the ground began to shake. A low rumbling sound got louder and louder until . . .

KA-BAAAAAM!

The volcano erupted, sending Spider-Man and the canister flying. He shot his web at it.

"Got it! No thanks to that eruption interruption," he said. Spider-Man was so relieved to have the Gigantor Particles in his possession that he didn't notice he had landed—and was stuck—in a petri dish of honey!

"Well, this is a sticky situation," he said.

"Or a sweet one," Doctor Octopus laughed, suddenly upon him. "Good-bye, spider-fool!" he cried as he snatched the canister from Spider-Man's gooey hand and ran.

Chapter 8

Doctor Octopus headed for the exit. If he made it outside before the heroes caught him, he could disappear. Then he—and the Gigantor Particles—would be gone for good!

Spider-Man tried to run forward through the honey, but it was like pushing against the waves at the beach. If only he could use the thickness of the sweet nectar to his advantage, like how he'd harnessed the power of the water's current in his science project.

A lightbulb went off over Spidey's head! He knew exactly what to do.

Ant-Man and the Wasp arrived to pull him free. As they tugged, Spider-Man said, "I know you guys are Avengers and all, but I think I know how to catch Doctor Octopus."

"Tell us your big idea, kid," Ant-Man said.

"Ant-Man, grab that spoon and stick it in the honey," Spider-Man instructed.

Ant-Man shoved the handle of the utensil into the thick amber goop.

"Wasp, can you pull the top part back as far as possible?"

"I sure can," the Wasp replied. She flew to the tip of the spoon, bent it all the way backward, and held it there.

Spider-Man climbed into the bowl of the makeshift catapult and curled himself into a ball. "Here goes nothing," he said. He gave the Wasp a thumbs-up. She let go.

Spider-Man catapulted into the air with such force that it didn't take long for him to reach Doctor Octopus and knock him to the ground. The Super

Villain went sprawling, and the canister
fell from his hand. It smashed open.
The Gigantor Particles spilled all over
them both.

"Oh no!" Spidey cried.

"Oh yes!" Doc Ock replied.

"We're going to be giants," they said
in unison.

As the particles took hold, the
Super Hero and the Super Villain grew
and grew and grew until . . . they were
back to their normal size.

"Huh," said Spider-Man. "The giant version of tiny us is regular-size us. That's a lesson in proportion."

"You fool!" cried Doctor Octopus. "You've ruined everything!"

Spider-Man shrugged. "And I'd say I saved the world. We'll just have to agree to disagree."

Doctor Octopus shot a tentacle at Spider-Man, knocking him off his feet. "I don't need to be huge to exterminate you irritating insects!" he cried. "Or to destroy the entire university!" Doctor Octopus began rampaging through the science fair.

Ant-Man and the Wasp returned to their regular size. They helped Spider-Man to his feet.

"We have to stop him," Ant-Man said.

"I've got it," the Wasp cried. She pointed to Flash's science project and the glass case that housed his ants. "All we have to do is break this open and we've got ourselves an army!"

"On it," Ant-Man said. He raised his
fist and was about to smash the case
when Spider-Man snatched it away.

"I'm sorry," Spidey said. "But I can't
let you do that."

"Oh no," said Ant-Man. "Did Doc Ock do some sort of mind control on you? I hate it when the bad guys do mind control."

"No, it's not that," Spider-Man said. "It's just that this is someone's science fair project and I know he worked really hard on it. I'd feel bad if we destroyed it."

"But Ant-Man can use neurotransmitters from his helmet to communicate with the ants," the Wasp explained. "He can send them into Doctor Octopus's metal arms so they can chew through the wires he uses to control them. The battle would be over in an instant."

"Really?" asked Spider-Man. "Wow, that *is* an awesome plan." He pictured Flash and all the hard work he had done. He shook his head. "But no. We can't."

"Sure you can," said a voice from behind a table. Flash Thompson popped his head out. "Those are my ants. If they can help stop Doctor Octopus, then they're all yours, Spider-Man."

"Are you sure?" Spidey asked. "Your project would be ruined."

Flash shrugged. "It's no biggie. The guy next to me with that awesome water project is probably going to win the trophy anyway. At least now my ants will be doing some good. I knew they were the coolest insects!"

Ant-Man smiled.

"No offense, Spider-Man," Flash said.

"None taken," answered Spidey.

"And listen," Flash added. "If you want to chew through wires, use the trap-jaw ants. Their mandibles move crazy fast, like a hundred and forty miles per hour. They'll get the job done in a snap."

Spider-Man was impressed. "And here I thought a spider bite was intense."

The Wasp cleared her throat. "Can we get back to beating the bad guy?" she asked.

Spidey nodded.

The Wasp smashed a hole into one side of the glass case.

Ant-Man sent a signal to the trap-jaw ants. In seconds they came streaming from the case and swarmed Doctor Octopus's metal arms. Then they disappeared inside the sockets.

"What is this?" Doc Ock laughed. "You think some tiny, insignificant ants are worthy adversaries for me?"

Spider-Man, Ant-Man, and the Wasp waited.

"I'll show you what real might is!" the villain continued. He raised his tentacles and prepared to bring them down on the three heroes. But before he could, there was a spark and some smoke. His metal arms went limp.

"My arms!" Doctor Octopus cried. "What have you done?"

"That's called short-circuiting," Ant-Man said. The trap-jaw ants streamed out of the tentacles and returned to his side.

"And these are called web-shooters," Spider-Man added. He tied the tentacles together with his webs.

"And this is known as a wasp sting," said the Wasp. She stunned Doctor Octopus with her stinger.

Then he fell at last, defeated, to the ground.

Chapter 10

Officer Stanley snapped the final handcuff shut. It was a special set of eight cuffs linked together by thick chains.

"And we just had this lying around in the squad car?" Officer Ditko asked his partner.

Officer Stanley nodded. "Two cuffs for the hands, two for the feet, and four for the metal arms," she said. She led Doctor Octopus out of the building and put him in the back of their police cruiser.

Spider-Man lowered himself
from the ceiling and addressed
Officer Ditko. "Just when you
think you've seen it all, am I
right?" he said.

Officer Ditko did a double
take. Then he shook his head and
followed his partner outside.

Spider-Man swung over to Ant-Man and the Wasp. "I'm sorry I spilled your Gigantor Particles," Spidey said.

"No worries," replied the Wasp. "We figured it out once. We'll do it again. And maybe this time we'll make it Super Villain–proof."

Ant-Man added, "I'm sorry we made you tiny."

"No big deal," said Spider-Man. "It was actually pretty cool to see things from your perspective. I used to think the bigger the better. But I guess not

always. I mean, look at how tough those ants were!"

"Never underestimate the little guy," Ant-Man agreed.

"Or the big guy," the Wasp added. "There's usually more to people than what you see on the surface."

Spider-Man looked over to where Aunt May was helping Flash clean up his broken science fair project. "There sure is," he agreed. Then he said good-bye to his super pals and swung out of sight.

Chapter 11

Despite the destruction caused by
Doctor Octopus, the science fair carried
on. Soon it was time to announce
the winner of the Big Apple Science
Trophy. Peter could barely contain his
excitement. He stood beside his project,
squeezing Aunt May's hand.

"And the trophy goes to . . ." The head judge opened an envelope. "Peter Parker."

The crowd of scientists, students, and their families applauded. Peter hugged his aunt. He walked to the front of the room to claim his prize. "Thank you," he said to the crowd. "This trophy means a lot to me. But if it's okay with the judges, I'd like to share it with someone else."

Peter pointed to Flash Thompson.

"I got to see Flash's ant project before it was destroyed tonight. And I can tell you it was really good. But even more impressive? It was Flash's project that saved the day. I heard that when Spider-Man, Ant-Man, and the Wasp needed Flash's ants to defeat Doctor Octopus, Flash said yes. He even told them which ants to use, which was some quick and smart thinking. For that, he deserves this award as much as I do."

The crowd cheered. Flash joined Peter at the front of the room and shook his hand, a giant smile on his face.

After the ceremony, Flash pulled Peter aside. "Thanks for including me, Parker," he said. "It means a lot that a smart guy like you thinks I did a good job."

Peter looked at his feet. "To tell you the truth," he said, "I didn't expect you

to make such a good project. I thought you were only interested in sports. I'm sorry I judged you, Flash. I promise not to do that again."

Flash considered this. "So does this mean there's more to you than just being a supersmart guy? Have you got some mad basketball skills I don't know about?"

Peter laughed. "Next time we have PE, pick me first and you'll find out."

"You've got it, Parker," Flash said. He and Peter walked toward the exit, where Aunt May was waiting for them with their projects. "Hey, why don't we meet at the courts this weekend and practice some one-on-one?"

Peter smiled. He'd learned a lot today, and not just about ants. "You're on," he said.

Sand Trap!

With Spider-Man, Squirrel Girl, and the Sandman

By **Mackenzie Cadenhead**
& Sean Ryan

Illustrated by **Dario Brizuela**

Los Angeles
New York

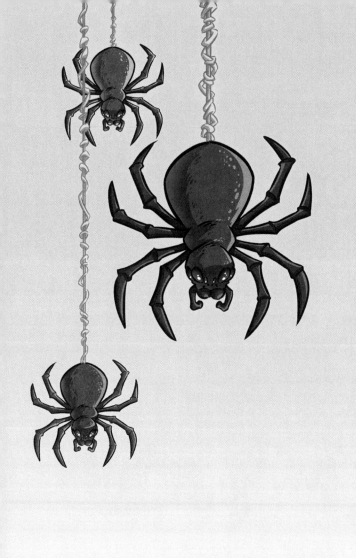

Chapter 1

Peter Parker did not hear his Aunt May talking. He had been pouring the last of the milk into his cereal bowl when the morning news caught his attention.

". . . commotion at the City Bank on Ninety-sixth Street and Columbus Avenue. Police cars are at the scene."

"Peter," Aunt May said again. She shook his shoulder. "Did you hear a word I just said?"

"Sorry, Aunt May," Peter replied.

He looked away from the TV. Aunt May's arms were crossed. *Uh-oh.*

Aunt May was the kindest person Peter knew. She had raised him since he was a little boy. She loved him as much as any parent could. Aunt May was friendly to everyone. And she always threw the ball back when the neighborhood kids lost it over her fence. When Aunt May wasn't smiling, something was wrong.

"Sorry for what?" she asked. "For paying more attention to the television than to your dearest aunt? Or for finishing the milk I asked you to save for my tea party?"

Peter looked at the Cheerios floating in the milk. "Oops," he said. "I forgot."

"Did you also forget that our neighbor Anna is bringing her niece over for tea later?" she asked. "Honestly, Peter. I think you might forget your own name if I didn't call it all the time."

It was true that Peter Parker often forgot to do the things his aunt asked. But it was not for the reason she thought. You see, Peter Parker had a lot on his mind. Peter Parker had a secret.

Peter Parker was Spider-Man!

And sometimes being Spider-Man made being Peter tough.

He looked at his frowning aunt.

I will not be Spider-Man today, he thought. Today I am just Peter Parker. I will be the perfect host for Aunt May's tea party. I will cut the lawn. I will clean my room. I will not get distracted. And I will *not* disappear.

Peter opened his mouth to say all this—except the part about being Spider-Man. But before he could speak, the TV news anchor said something he could not ignore.

"There appears to be a man made of sand leaving the bank with bags full of money. And what do I see? Just like sand through your fingers, this Sandman has slipped past the police! He's headed for Central Park with patrol cars in pursuit! Can anyone stop this powdery plunderer? Or will we bury our heads in the sand as he gets away?"

Chapter 2

"I'll be back with the milk before you know it," Peter said. He stepped onto the sidewalk outside their house in Queens, New York.

"Just to the store, Peter," Aunt May warned from the front door. "Please try not to be late for our guests."

Peter gave his aunt a thumbs-up. He turned the corner and was gone.

It was a bright spring afternoon. Perfect weather for going to the grocery store. Or . . . for sailing through the air on a spiderweb!

"Woo-hoo!" Spider-Man yelled as he swung between skyscrapers. "The Sandman was last seen headed toward Central Park. I bet I can make it there in a New York minute!"

Spider-Man raced into Manhattan. He knew he must catch the Sandman quickly if he wanted to make his tea time.

There was no question that Peter wanted to help Aunt May. He *wanted* to get the milk—he could swing by the grocery store on his way home. He even *wanted* to go to the tea party—everyone

likes a nice cup of Earl Grey, right? But after he was bitten by a radioactive spider and woke up with super powers, Peter had learned that sometimes the tea parties had to wait.

So it was for the webbed warrior. Spider-Man's super heroics were always in demand. Still, having a secret Super Hero identity was not always easy. He could hardly tell his teachers that the Green Goblin ate his homework.

But whenever Peter wondered if

he should hang up his webs and leave crime fighting to the Avengers, the words of his late Uncle Ben helped him make the right choice. "With great power comes great responsibility," Uncle Ben had told him.

No matter what was happening in Peter Parker's world, Spider-Man would always answer a call for help!

Chapter 3

"There is sand everywhere! In my shoes, my pockets, everywhere!" Officer Ditko said to his partner, Officer Stanley. Their police car raced down the street. They were in hot pursuit of the criminal who had just robbed a bank.

"We're trying to catch the Sandman!" Officer Stanley yelled back. "What did you expect? A day at the beach?!"

As if in answer to her question, an enormous wave of sand crashed down in front of them. Ninety-sixth Street was a sand trap. Officer Stanley hit the gas, but the

police car's wheels would not budge. They were stuck. The Sandman had escaped!

Officer Ditko spat sand from his mouth. He looked at his partner. "You had to ask," he said.

As the police officers searched the sand for their suspect, the Sandman ran into Central Park.

"Why can't they just leave me alone?" the Sandman asked himself. "I only took a few thousand dollars. My doctor says that after getting fired from so many jobs, I've got a lot of stress. She says I need a vacation. She says I should find a nice sandy beach where I can pull myself back together."

The Sandman looked at the bags of cash he held in his fists. "Speaking of getting away, I need a place to hide until all of this blows over."

The crumbly crook surveyed his surroundings.

Trees? Nope.

Dog park? No thank you.

Playground? The Sandman smiled.

In front of him was a giant playground with swings, slides, and a very welcoming sandbox. "The cops will never find me there!" he said.

Only one thing stood between him and his hideout. The sandbox was full of cheerful children and caring caregivers. He had to distract them. The Sandman shape-shifted his mouth into a bullhorn and shouted, "ICE CREAM!"

The children cheered. Their parents applauded. Everyone ran from the sandbox in pursuit of the ice cream truck! And as they searched for the

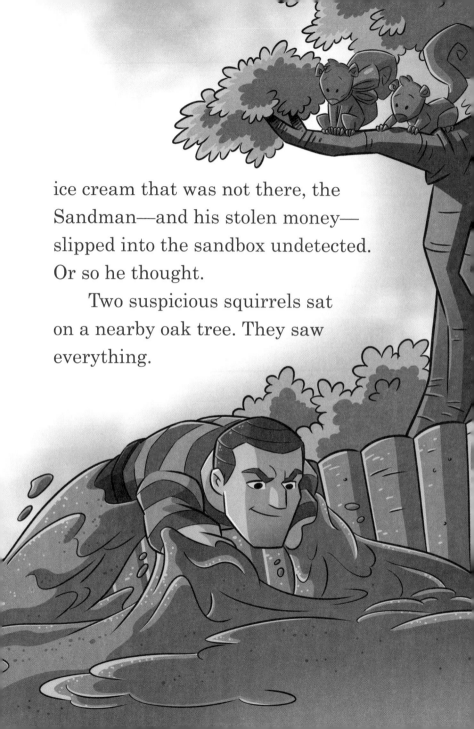

ice cream that was not there, the Sandman—and his stolen money—slipped into the sandbox undetected. Or so he thought.

Two suspicious squirrels sat on a nearby oak tree. They saw everything.

Chapter 4

"The Sandman's here? No way!"
A girl with big front teeth and a bushy
brown tail sat on a park bench speaking
to a squirrel.

"Chitik chit chik," the squirrel
replied. She placed her tiny squirrel
hands on her hips and scowled.

"Oh, I totally believe you, Tippy-
Toe," Squirrel Girl said to her squirrel
friend. "I'm just glad we finally have
something to do. Today has been
D-U-double-L DULL! I was so bored

that I counted how many acorns I could fit in my cheeks. Made me wonder what I was doing with my life. You know?"

Tippy-Toe shrugged.

"Forty-seven, by the way." Squirrel Girl leaped from the bench to a nearby tree. "But enough about me," she said. "Tell me about you. Where did you last see this Sandman?"

Squirrel Girl and Tippy-Toe took to the treetops. The little furry rodent told her larger furry friend everything she had seen. This was a good choice on Tippy-Toe's part because Squirrel Girl was a Super Hero.

Having an awesome tail and being able to talk to squirrels was just the beginning of Squirrel Girl's amazing abilities. Her strength was super. Her speed was super. Her quick reflexes were super. Her buck teeth were so strong they could chew through wood— and that was super! Even her real name was super, because it rhymed. (Doreen Green. Say *that* three times fast.)

Squirrel Girl and Tippy-Toe sat in the trees above the playground where the Sandman lay hidden. Squirrel Girl paused.

Having found no ice cream, the children had returned to the playground where the Sandman was hiding. This complicated Squirrel Girl's job. She had to fight the Sandman. She had to find the stolen money. She had to keep the kids safe. It was a lot to do on her own. Her teeth began to chitter nervously.

Then she saw something that made her smile. Suspended from a spiderweb, hanging upside down from a tree, was Spider-Man. He was talking with two police officers.

"Tippy-Toe, gather some squirrel friends," Squirrel Girl said. "I've got a bug to catch."

Chapter 5

Officer Ditko sneezed. Sand flew out of his nose, spraying the front of his uniform. "See? It's everywhere," the policeman whined.

Spider-Man patted him on the back. "I totally under-*sand*," Spidey said.

Officer Stanley shook her head. "More importantly, we cannot find the Sandman anywhere. Believe me, we've looked."

She pointed to a dozen police officers. They were sifting through the sand that covered Ninety-sixth Street. She held up a shovel. "Back to work," she said.

Officer Ditko sighed. He picked up a comb and fell to his knees. "If you see something, say something, okay, Spidey?"

"Will do, Officer," Spider-Man said. "Don't worry. This guy doesn't *sand* a chance."

Officer Ditko whimpered. "I'm too old for this—"

"Psst!"

Spider-Man looked behind him. He looked beside him. He looked below him. He was sure he heard something, but he saw nothing.

"Psst!" He heard it again.

Was the sound coming from the trees? Spidey looked up. Sitting on a branch in the tree above, a grinning girl with full cheeks and really big front teeth waved.

"Hi there!" she said. "It is great to meet you. Big fan. I totally love your vibe. Like the web-shooters. LOVE the puns. You fight all the best villains, and you do it with such style. I mean, for real, do you have a day job? Because if you wanted to perform at kids' birthday parties you would totally clean up."

Spider-Man was confused. "And you are?"

Squirrel Girl smacked her forehead with the palm of her hand. "Duh!" she said. "I'm Squirrel Girl!"

"Squirrel Girl?" Spidey chuckled. "Like, you have the powers of a squirrel?"

Squirrel Girl narrowed her eyes. She snapped a dead branch off the tree and did a double flip onto the sidewalk. Landing lightly on her feet, she said, "Along with the powers of a girl. You got a problem with that, bug-boy?"

"I do not," Spider-Man replied. He held out his hand. Squirrel Girl gave him a high five. "So, SG, any chance you've seen a—"

"Big guy made of sand?" Squirrel Girl asked eagerly. "You betcha. Follow me!"

Chapter 6

Spider-Man and Squirrel Girl stood in the center of the playground.

"I thought you said he was hiding in a sandbox," Spider-Man said.

"He is," Squirrel Girl replied. "Did I forget to mention that the whole playground is covered in sand?"

Spider-Man rubbed his temples. Just as Tippy-Toe had said, the Sandman had hidden in the sandy area meant for burying toys and building castles. But the fact that the rest of the

playground had a sand floor, too, was not good news.

"The Sandman could be hiding anywhere," Spider-Man said. "Under the tire swing. Beneath the slide. We have to get these kids out of here. And I know just how to do it." He winked at his companion. "Watch and learn." Spider-Man cleared his throat. He cupped his hands around his mouth. He hollered, "ICE CREAM!"

Everyone stopped playing. The children glared. Their parents pouted. No one moved.

"Geesh," Spidey said. "Not a big ice cream crowd."

"That was a great try, Spider-Man,"

Squirrel Girl said. She patted him kindly on the shoulder. "But I am Central Park's protector. And if there's one thing I know, it's how to clear a playground." She looked into the trees. "Ready, Tippy-Toe?"

"Chitik!" a tiny voice replied.

Squirrel Girl placed her fingers in her mouth on either side of her amazing front teeth. She whistled.

Hundreds of squirrels ran into the playground. They descended from the trees. They scurried over rocks. They burst forth from bushes. Gray squirrels,

black squirrels, red squirrels.
All the squirrels in Central Park
seemed to have come at Squirrel
Girl's call.

Now, one squirrel on its own
is cute. Two squirrels playing
together can be entertaining. But
hundreds of them rushing at you
in formation is simply nuts.

The families fled to the nearby
benches. The squirrels stood

guard at their feet. The playground was cleared and not a moment too soon.

A huge figure grew out of the sand. He loomed above Spider-Man and Squirrel Girl.

"Playtime's over, kids."

Chapter 7

Aunt May placed a small spoon on top of a neatly folded napkin. She centered a teacup in its saucer. She laid eight cookies on a fancy silver tray. Her tea party was nearly ready.

All that was missing was the milk.

"Oh, I do hope Peter will be back from the store soon," she said to herself. "Anna and her niece will be here any minute."

Having nothing to do but wait, Aunt May decided to distract herself.

She turned on the TV. She raised the volume.

"Breaking news from Central Park," the newscaster said. "The Sandman has been spotted at a local playground. Though there is no sign yet of the stolen money, Spider-Man has arrived on the scene."

Aunt May forgot her dairy dilemma. How could one think of milk when Spider-Man was on the news? Had Aunt May known that Spider-Man was actually her nephew, Peter, she would not have been excited about this fight. But Aunt May did not know. And Aunt May thought Spider-Man was wonderful. He had good character and a good heart. She was glad to have him on her side, fighting bad guys and keeping New York safe. She was also delighted to see he had a friend with him to help.

". . . received word that Squirrel Girl has joined Spidey in the fight. Will this terrific twosome pound sand, or will they draw a line in it? Either way, one thing is certain: this battle will be no picnic."

Aunt May grabbed a cookie. "Get him, Spider-Man," she said as she took a bite.

Chapter 8

"The lady only said to give the dog a walk," the Sandman whined. "She never said anything about bringing him back. I don't think I should've been fired for that." The Sandman chased Squirrel Girl up a ladder. She shot down a tunnel slide. He followed.

"And that gave you the right to rob the bank—why?" Squirrel Girl asked. "Seriously, dude. You absolutely deserved to be fired from that job. Poor puppy!" Squirrel Girl tumbled out of the

tunnel and ducked. Thousands of grains of sand came flying out after her. They landed in a heap by the swing set where Spider-Man was waiting.

"Excuses, excuses," Spidey said. "What's next? Someone hired you to watch their kids and then fired you for no good reason?"

The pile of sand pulled together. It formed into the Sandman. He faced

Spider-Man and shrugged. "They wouldn't even hire me. If I'm not supposed to do it, then don't call it baby *sitting*," he said.

Spider-Man gasped. "Now that's just wrong."

The Sandman lunged at the wall-crawler. Spidey jumped onto a tire swing.

"You know what they say, don't you?" Spider-Man asked. He swung forward. He was about to hit the Sandman when the thief turned himself to dust. Spider-Man went straight through him.

"Don't stand in front of swings or you might get hit," the Sandman said as he returned to solid form. He clenched his fists. He waited for Spider-Man to swing backward. But the swing and Spidey never came.

"I was thinking, what goes around comes around," Spider-Man said. He had shot his webs onto the frame of the swing set, and was squatting at the top. Now he pulled himself all the way around. He hit the Sandman from behind.

"Oof!" The felon went flying onto the monkey bars.

"No fair," the Sandman cried. "I wasn't expecting that."

"So you want us to tell you when we're going to fight you?" Squirrel Girl asked. She was perched atop the monkey bars. The Sandman looked up at her.

"Why, yes," he said.

"Okay." Squirrel Girl smiled. "Incoming!"

At Squirrel Girl's call, nearly a dozen squirrels climbed the monkey bars to meet her. Their cheeks were full. They were stuffed with acorns. They faced the Sandman and blew.

"Ouch, ouch, ouch!" the Sandman cried. The squirrels pelted him with acorn after acorn. The attack was working. The Sandman

stumbled backward. Spider-Man was
waiting behind him. He held out a huge
net made of spiderwebs to contain the
crook.

Squirrel Girl smiled at Spidey.

The Sandman saw her look.

Before Spidey could catch him, the Sandman spun around and walloped the web-slinger. *Wham!*

Spider-Man went flying. He landed at the foot of a water fountain, where a little boy was filling up water balloons. A moment later, Squirrel Girl landed there, too.

Chapter
9

Phinneas Daniels had already had two warnings today. The first was after he dropped a water balloon on his mother's shoes (an accident). The second was after he dropped one on his little sister's head (not an accident). If

his water balloons made contact with one more person, they would be taken away. That was his mother's promise.

So Phinn had decided to fill up every last one of his balloons with water. That way, when he drenched his dad with all the balloons he had left, there wouldn't be any to take away. Phinn understood he was a genius.

Eighteen of Phinn's nineteen balloons were filled and sitting in his red wagon. He was about to fill the

last one when a million or so squirrels stormed the playground. Most of the playground players had jumped onto benches. A few climbed the fence. Phinn leaped up onto the water fountain. He did not know that he had landed on the fountain's push button. Nor did he know that he was causing water to trickle out. At first, he was distracted by the three tough-looking squirrels below him. After that, he was too busy watching a real live Super Hero fight.

Then Spider-Man and Squirrel Girl came flying through the air and landed next to Phinn. He was so surprised that he did not realize Spider-Man was talking to him.

"What?" Phinn asked.

"I said, wasting water is kind of rude, dude," Spider-Man repeated.

"Slow the flow, save H2O." He pointed at the water coming from the fountain.

"Oh, sorry," said Phinn. He shifted his weight off the button.

"Chitta chit!" barked one of the red squirrels below.

"It's okay, Buddy," Squirrel Girl replied. "We'll rinse you off when the battle's done."

Phinn looked at the squirrel, who was covered in wet, sandy glop.

"Hey, Spidey. Wasting water also gets Buddy muddy," Phinn said. He hoped the Super Hero would appreciate his rhyme. Maybe give him a thumbs-up.

What he got was way better.

"That's it!" Squirrel Girl said. "The water! Kid, you're a genius!"

Phinn beamed. He didn't know what Squirrel Girl was talking about, but it was nice that someone appreciated his smarts.

"Can we borrow your balloons?" Spider-Man asked. Phinn nodded. The Super Heroes took the red wagon into battle. Phinn picked up Buddy the squirrel and rinsed him off. Then he filled up balloon nineteen, just in case.

Chapter
10

"Thanks for the workout, web-head," the Sandman said. "But it's time my money and I got going." The Sandman reached his hand into the sandbox. He pulled out the bags of cash. He took a step toward the playground's exit.

"So soon?" said Spider-Man. "But Squirrel Girl was just getting to know you."

The Sandman spun around. He glared at Spider-Man, who was standing just beyond the big slide. "I told you to stay put," the Sandman said. "Guess the only way to stop a spider is to squash it."

The Sandman charged at Spider-Man.

Spidey didn't move.

The Sandman got closer.

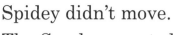

Spidey stood still.

The Sandman kept coming and coming until he was only a few feet away from the web-slinger.

Spider-Man stood his ground. But when the Sandman reached the bottom of the slide, Spidey shouted, "Balloons away!"

Squirrel Girl sprang from the top of the big slide. Phinn's red wagon was next to her. "Hey, you dusty dope!" she called. "No one messes with my park!" Squirrel Girl sent an armful of water balloons tumbling down the slide.

The first water balloon hit the Sandman on the foot. The second one landed on his thigh. The third burst against his knee. The fourth, fifth,

sixth, and seventh followed fast. And the water from the balloons turned the Sandman's lower body into mud.

"Wha-what's happening to me?" the Sandman cried. "I can't move!"

"What's the matter, Sandy?" Spider-Man asked as the rest of the eighteen water balloons burst against the bad guy. "Or should I call you Stucky?"

"Why, you little—" The Sandman raised his hand. His fist became a hammer. He pulled his arm back. He was about to nail Spidey when a water balloon went whizzing through the air. It hit the hammer head-on and exploded. The Sandman's hand turned to mush.

Spider-Man turned to see where the balloon had come from. Phinn stood beside the water fountain. He smiled and waved. Buddy the squirrel was on his shoulder. Spidey gave them a thumbs-up.

Chapter 11

Officer Stanley shoveled the last of the mud-caked Sandman into an extra-extra-extra-large Ziploc bag.

"I mean, who needs the attendance monitor to show up on time?" the Sandman asked her. "Isn't it the kids who can't be late? I don't think I should have been fired for that."

Officer Ditko sealed the plastic bag shut, but the Sandman's sweater got caught in the zipper. The pullover went poof, leaving Officer Ditko covered in sand.

"Everywhere," the policeman sighed.

"Thanks for the help, Spider-Man and Squirrel Girl," Officer Stanley said. She loaded the bagged-and-tagged Sandman into the police van.

"No thanks necessary," Spidey replied. "We don't do it for the applause. No need for a *sand*-ing ovation."

Just then the children from the playground came running toward Spider-Man and Squirrel Girl. They were cheering. They were clapping. They were shouting for joy.

"Well, maybe just this once," Spidey said. He held out his arms. Squirrel Girl prepared for high fives. The children ran up to them—and zoomed right past them to the ice cream truck that had finally arrived.

"At least they have their priorities straight," Squirrel Girl said. "To thank you for your help  in protecting my park, may I buy you a cone, Spider-Man? What kind of ice cream do you like? Vanilla? Chocolate? Coffee?"

"Definitely not coffee," he replied. "I'm actually more of a tea man, myself."

Spider-Man froze. Tea, he thought. He was late for Aunt May's tea party!

"Squirrel Girl, I'm sorry to fight crime and fly, but I'm an hour past late for something really important," he explained. "Can I take a rain check on that celebration?"

"Sure thing, bug-boy," Squirrel Girl said. "You're welcome in Central Park anytime. Right, Tippy-Toe?"

"Chitta chit," Tippy-Toe agreed.

Spider-Man gave Central Park's protector and her squirrely sidekick a nod. Then he took to the skies.

Chapter 12

Peter Parker stared at his front door. In one hand he held his house keys. In the other, he held a carton of milk. He took a deep breath, unlocked the door, and went inside.

"Aunt May," he called. "I'm back."

There was no response. All the lights in the house were out except for those in the kitchen. He could hear water running. He followed the sound.

Aunt May was cleaning the last of the teacups in the sink. She set it to dry alongside the others. She turned off the water.

"I brought the milk," Peter said. He did not look at Aunt May. Instead, he looked at his feet.

"Thank you, Peter," Aunt May said. "We can use it for breakfast tomorrow."

Peter looked up. "Tomorrow?" he asked. "But the tea party—?"

"Is over," she said. "Anna and her niece left early."

Peter's face flushed red. If only he could tell Aunt May he was Spider-Man. She would understand why he was late

with the milk and he wouldn't have to feel so guilty. Then Peter had an idea. While he couldn't tell Aunt May that he was a Super Hero, he could tell her that being late wasn't his fault!

"You know," Peter said, "I would have been back with the milk right away but I ran into a friend who needed my help. I couldn't say no because she was really in a sandy— I mean, sticky situation. And just when I thought the problem was solved, it got even bigger! How was I supposed to know that was going to happen?"

Peter stopped talking. His words reminded him of ones he had heard earlier. They sounded like the words the Sandman had used to excuse his bad behavior. Peter went to Aunt May and took her hands.

"But none of that matters, Aunt May," he said. "There's no excuse for missing the tea party. And there's no excuse for not bringing you the milk when I said I would. I'm sorry I ruined your day. I hope you can forgive me."

Aunt May hugged her nephew. "Thank you, Peter," she said. "I accept your apology. I am proud of you for taking responsibility."

She walked to the dish-drying rack and pulled out two teacups. "But nothing is ruined. Early evening is a perfect time for tea."

Peter smiled. "I'll turn on the kettle," he said. He grabbed the teapot on the stove and filled it with water from the sink.

"Would you please get two saucers for the cups, as well?" Aunt May asked. She pulled out a box of tea.

"You betcha," Peter replied. Together, they set the kitchen table for a tea party for two.

Peter Parker and his aunt enjoyed a nice cup of Earl Grey tea with milk. She told him about Spider-Man's exciting adventure that she had watched on the news. He made sure her cup was never empty.

As Peter and Aunt May drank their tea, two squirrels perched on a branch just outside the Parkers' kitchen window. They watched the tea party in the evening light. They chittered away and enjoyed an acorn feast of their own.